Ogre Eats Everything

DEAR OGRE,
I LIKE YOU
your
friend
MAYBE

⊙⊙ by Bethany Roberts ⊙⊙

⊙⊙ pictures by Marsha Winborn ⊙⊙

DUTTON CHILDREN'S BOOKS · NEW YORK

To Lucia,
for her insight and enthusiasm
—B.R.

CIP Data is available.

Published in the United States by Dutton Children's Books,
a division of Penguin Young Readers Group
345 Hudson Street, New York, New York 10014
www.penguin.com
Designed by Irene Vandervoort
Manufactured in China   First Edition
ISBN 0-525-47291-6
1   3   5   7   9   10   8   6   4   2

Contents

One spring morning,

Ogre woke up late.

He looked out the window.

May Belle was working in the garden.

While she worked, she sang:

"Red and yellow

In a row.

Little tulips,

Grow, grow, grow!"

Ogre skipped into the kitchen.

BUMP! CLUMP! KA-THUMP!

He was hungry!

Ogre ate all the cereal.

He ate all the toast.

He drank all the milk.

But he was still hungry.

"Oo-oo-ooh, pretty flowers!

Yum!" said Ogre.

May Belle came into the kitchen.

She saw boxes and bags

and bottles.

They were all empty.

Then she looked out the window.

ᬑ 9 ᬑ

Ogre was eating the tulips!

"STOP!" May Belle cried.

"Tulips are NOT for eating!"

May Belle put out her hands.

But it was too late.

"Now you must plant

a *new* garden," she said.

"Oo-oo-ooh!" said Ogre.

"Dig!" said May Belle.

Ogre dug.

"Plant!" said May Belle.

Ogre planted.

Soon the garden began to grow.

They watered …

and weeded …

and waited …

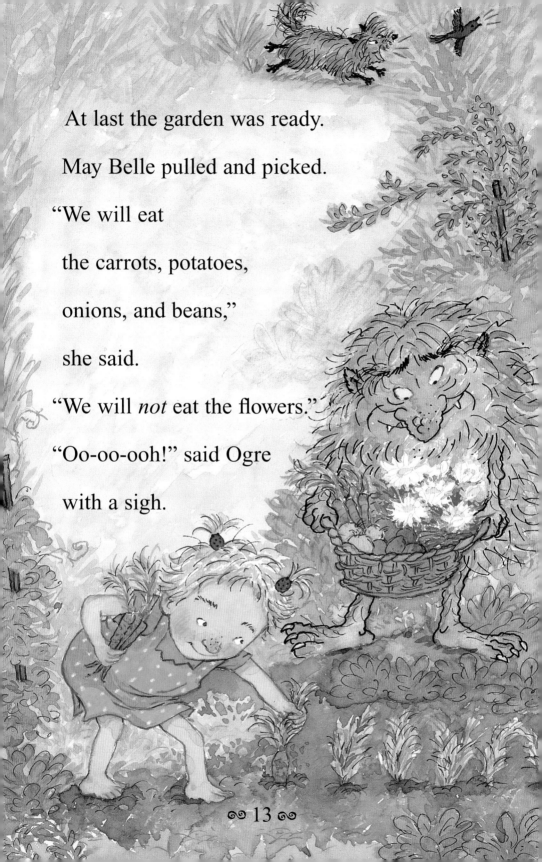

At last the garden was ready.

May Belle pulled and picked.

"We will eat

the carrots, potatoes,

onions, and beans,"

she said.

"We will *not* eat the flowers."

"Oo-oo-ooh!" said Ogre

with a sigh.

∞ 13 ∞

May Belle cooked a fine stew.

She put bowls of stew on the table.

She put flowers on the table, too.

"Time to eat," she said. "Dig in!"

They ate the stew all up.

Yum! It was good.

Ogre was still hungry.

Ogre looked at the flowers.

He rubbed his belly.

He smacked his lips.

"Oo-oo-ooh!" he said.

"Flowers look good."

"You may have *one* flower,"

said May Belle.

Ogre grinned.

Ogre ate one flower.

Yum!

One afternoon,

Ogre got a note.

It was from May Belle.

Ogre looked at the note.

He looked at it upside down.

He scratched his head.

Then he ate the note.

"No, no," said May Belle.

"That note was to read, not to eat.

The note said: 'Come to tea at 2:00.'

We will have a tea party!"

Ogre grinned.

"I will teach you to read
at our tea party," said May Belle.
"So the next time you get a note,
you will read it, not eat it."

BUMP!

CLUMP!

KA-THUMP!

Ogre jumped up and down.
"Oo-oo-ooh!" he said.

"We must dress up
for our tea party,"
said May Belle.
May Belle and Ogre
put on fancy hats
and gloves and beads.

May Belle took a piece of paper.

She wrote H-A-T.

"That spells *hat*," she said.

"Hat," said Ogre.

Ogre looked at the paper.

He looked at his hat.

Ogre put the note on his head.

"No, no," said May Belle.

"That note is to read,

not to put on your head."

"Oo-oo-ooh!" said Ogre.

"We must have flowers

on the table," said May Belle.

They picked some flowers.

May Belle wrote F-L-O-W-E-R.

"That spells *flower*," she said.

"Flower," said Ogre.

Ogre looked at the paper.

He looked at a flower.

Ogre sniffed the note.

"No, no," said May Belle.

"That note is to read,

not to sniff."

"Oo-oo-ooh!" said Ogre.

"And now," said May Belle,

"we need fancy tea for our tea party."

May Belle made some fancy apple tea.

She took two teacups

from the cupboard.

Then May Belle wrote C-U-P.

"That spells *cup*," said May Belle.

"Cup," said Ogre.

Ogre looked at the paper.

He looked at his cup.

Ogre tried to drink from the note.

"No, no," said May Belle.

"That note is to read,

not to drink from."

"Oo-oo-ooh!" said Ogre.

"We will have our tea in the garden,"

said May Belle.

They carried the tea, the flowers,

some bread, and a jar of jam

out to the garden.

They sat under a shady tree.

They drank their tea.

Ogre slurped.

They ate their bread and jam.

Ogre burped.

YUM!

Then May Belle put her finger

in the jam jar.

She wrote J-A-M on Ogre's plate.

"That spells *jam*," said May Belle.

Ogre looked at his plate.

He looked at the jam.

He looked at his plate again.

"JAM," read Ogre.

"JAM, JAM, JAM, JAM,

JAM, JAM, JAM!"

"You are reading!" said May Belle.

"Good for you!"

BUMP!

CLUMP!

KA-THUMP!

Then May Belle and Ogre sang a song.

"Read it, read it,

Doo-wacka-doo.

Jam for me,

Jam for you!

J-A-M spells JAM!"

Ogre read every day.

One day, he read a soup can.

Another day, he read his cereal box.

Another day, he read the honey jar.

And the next time May Belle gave him a note,

Ogre could read it . . .

         all by himself.

Ogre Is Bored

One day,

Ogre was bored.

There was nothing to do.

May Belle made a daisy chain.

She put it on his head.

Ogre ate the daisies.

But Ogre was still bored.

"Bah," he said.

May Belle picked some blueberries.

She gave them to Ogre.

Ogre ate the blueberries.

He ate the basket, too.

But Ogre was still bored.

"Bah," he said.

"Come and smell a rose,"

called May Belle.

Ogre sniffed a rose.

Then he ate it.

But Ogre was still bored.

"Bah," he said.

"Try standing on your head,"

said May Belle.

Ogre stood on his head.

But he was still bored.

"Try spinning in circles,"

said May Belle.

Ogre spun in circles.

But he was still bored.

"Try bumping, clumping,

and ka-thumping,"

said May Belle.

Ogre bumped, clumped,

and ka-thumped.

He bumped, clumped,

and ka-thumped

right into a beehive.

BUZZZ! BUZZZ!
BUZZZ!

Suddenly,

bees buzzed out

from the beehive.

The bees buzzed after Ogre.

"OO-OO-OOH!" cried Ogre.

"Run, Ogre, run!"

cried May Belle.

Ogre ran.

The bees flew after him.

Ogre ran faster.

The bees flew faster.

"Jump into the pond, Ogre!"

cried May Belle.

Ogre jumped into the pond.

SPLASH!

"You can come out now,"

called May Belle.

"The bees have gone away."

Ogre came out of the pond.

Ogre was not bored anymore!

Ogre was all wet.

"Oo-oo-ooh!" he said.

"Come and dry off in the sunshine,"

said May Belle.

"We can paint pictures."

May Belle painted pictures of the garden.

As she painted, May Belle sang:

"Paint a picture

Of roses and bees,

Of sunshine and berries,

Of daisies and trees."

Ogre painted a picture.

He painted a picture of a bee.

Ogre ate the picture.

Then Ogre painted a picture

of two friends having fun in a garden.

He didn't eat this picture.

He gave it to May Belle.

"Thank you, Ogre," said May Belle.

"This is a great picture!"

May Belle wrote B-E-S-T F-R-I-E-N-D-S

on the picture.

Ogre grinned.

He jumped up and down.

BUMP! CLUMP! KA-THUMP!

And May Belle sang a song:

"Two best friends,

You and me.

Bees and tulips.

Jam and tea.

Two best friends,

Me and you.

Doo-wacka-doo,

Wacka-doo-wacka-doo!"

Arf!

Then Ogre and May Belle did

a best friends dance

in the garden together.

SHUFFLE, CLUMP!

BUMP!

SHUFFLE,

SWISH, SWISH, SWISH!

DOO-WACKA-DOO,

WACKA-DOO!